Created by Michael Bovill
Written by Alexandra Bovill

The Story of

TRACKER

santa's puppy

Illustrated by Jeff Roux

LandMarc
PRESS

Book design by LandMarc Press.

Illustration services provided by Brave River Solutions.

For general information on our other products and services or technical support, please contact LandMarc Press
at (936) 544-5137, fax (936) 544-2270, or on the web at
www.LandMarcPress.com.

ISBN 978-0-9797184-3-4

Printed in the United States of America.

10 9 8 7 6 5 4 3 2 1

List of Movie Stars in the Book:

Santa

Chase

Mrs. Claus

Tracker

Blitzen

Howie

Spencer

Santa opened his front door as he did every morning to sniff the fresh North Pole air and noticed Spencer the mail elf rushing up the path carrying a basket covered with a small red plaid blanket.

"Are those my favorite muffins?" Santa asked.

"I'm afraid not," Spencer said, grinning. "This basket came to the Post Office addressed to you! Wait until you see what it is!!!"

Santa lifted the corner of the blanket and peered underneath. To his surprise a little black nose popped out.

"Ho Ho Ho!" Santa laughed, his tummy jiggling. Under the blanket he saw two white floppy ears and two little black eyes that were staring up at him.

"It's a puppy!" Santa exclaimed. "Bring him inside and let him warm up by the fire."

Spencer carried the basket into the living room and set it on the carpet in front of the fireplace.

Mrs. Claus came into the living room to see who had arrived. She saw Spencer and then the basket covered with the little red plaid blanket and just knew it was full of muffins.

When the blanket began to move she stopped suddenly!

Why are our muffins moving, Santa?" she asked and before he could answer a little paw appeared, and then another, and finally the puppy was out of the basket, and standing in the living room.

He looked around and then at the three people staring at him before giving his fur a big shake.

"He is so adorable," said Mrs. Claus with a smile on her face and in her voice.

He is indeed," agreed Santa. "I have to tell the other elves and the reindeer and, well, everybody, about this!" Spencer said as he rushed out the door.

Santa and Mrs. Claus looked at each other and then at the puppy who had made himself right at home.

Just look at him, he looks so happy. I think he loves it here," Mrs. Claus said.

Santa thought this little fellow was special, but they didn't know yet that this particular puppy was very special indeed.

Spencer and the other elves, reindeer, and all the townsfolk gathered in the center of the village.

Santa and Mrs. Claus wrapped the puppy in his red plaid blanket and went to greet everyone.

We have a new addition to our North Pole family," Santa said as he gently unwrapped the blanket revealing the puppy.

Someone let out a gasp and cried, "Oh, he's so cute!"

"What's his name?" asked one of the elves.

I don't know," Santa replied as he placed the puppy on the snow-covered ground. "We'll have to think of one and find him a special job."

The puppy rolled in the snow and then shook himself. He stuck his nose into the snow and looked up at everyone...

Then the puppy began to give each elf a "hello" sniff. As he was running from elf to elf, Mrs. Claus noticed something peculiar: his ears kept flopping up and down.

Santa," she said, "look at his ears, they flop up and down. Do you think he's sick?" she asked.

"I'm not quite sure, but he doesn't seem to be," Santa replied. "He's very active and his eyes are bright and clear."

The elves were petting him as he ran to each one. Then he ran and sniffed "hello" to all the reindeer, too.

But, when he came to Blitzen, his left ear stood straight up!!

That's when Santa began to suspect what was happening.

You see, Santa knew that Blitzen had been a little naughty lately. He had gotten into the chocolate at the candy factory and had eaten too much.

Amazingly, when the puppy sniffed Blitzen the word Naughty appeared inside his left ear.

He's not sick my dear; he can tell if someone is naughty or nice by sniffing them! His nose is like a tracker," Santa said.

"I know that dogs have a wonderful sense of smell but this is quite unusual," said Mrs. Claus, "a puppy whose ears tell whether you are naughty or nice."

You're right, it is very unusual, and I have the perfect job for him. He can help me with my "Naughty or Nice" list. He'll be my tracker," said Santa.

"Why Santa I think you've found the perfect name for him, too!" Spencer exclaimed. "Tracker— you should name him Tracker."

"You're right Spencer, that is the only name for him," Santa agreed.

Everyone cheered, "Hooray for Tracker!!!!"

Visit Tracker's website at:

www.santaspuppy.com

For fun games and interactive adventures with Tracker, the elves, and Santa too!

Visit Tracker's great, kid-friendly website at:

www.santaspuppy.com

And look for new adventures of Tracker coming to a bookstore near you!